The Three Brothers

Original title:
The Three Brothers

Editor: Kristo Villem
ISBN 978-9916-676-79-0

The Three Brothers

By Clement Portlander

Dedicated to Gustav

"The Three Brothers" is a classic Estonian fairy tale that has been passed down through the generations. It tells the story of three brothers who are all skilled in different trades. The eldest brother is a blacksmith, the middle brother is a carpenter, and the youngest brother is a tailor.

One day, the three brothers decide to go on a journey to seek their fortunes. As they are traveling, they come across an old man who is being chased by a group of bandits. The brothers decide to help the old man and defeat the bandits, saving his life.

As a reward, the old man gives the brothers a magic bag that will grant them any wish they desire. The brothers are overjoyed and decide to use the bag to become wealthy and successful.

The eldest brother wishes for a forge that will produce the finest swords in the land. His wish is granted and he becomes a successful blacksmith. The middle brother wishes for a workshop that will produce the most beautiful furniture in the land. His wish is also granted and he becomes a successful carpenter.

The youngest brother, however, is not content with simply becoming wealthy. He wants to use his skills to help others and wishes for a magic needle that will sew clothes for the poor. His wish is granted and he becomes a beloved tailor who is known for his generosity and kindness.

The moral of this story is that wealth and success are not the most important things in life. The three brothers all achieved wealth and success, but it was the youngest brother who found true happiness by using his skills to help others.

This story serves as a reminder that we should not let our pursuit of material wealth and success overshadow our values and our desire to make a positive impact on the world. It teaches us that true happiness and fulfillment come from using our skills and talents to help others and make a difference in the world.

Overall, "The Three Brothers" is a timeless tale that has been passed down through the generations in Estonia. It is a story that reminds us of the importance of using our skills and talents to make a positive difference in the world. It is a story that will continue to inspire and educate people for generations to come, reminding us all of the value of compassion and selflessness in a world where these qualities are often in short supply.

Imagine a group of friends who are all struggling to find their passion and purpose in life. One friend, Lucy, is a talented graphic designer who spends her days working at a dull corporate job. Another friend, Jack, is a skilled carpenter who is tired of working for a boss who takes credit for his hard work. And the third friend, Sarah, is a kind-hearted nurse who wants to use her skills to make a difference in the world.

One day, the friends come across a magic lamp that grants them each a wish. Lucy wishes for a successful design business where she can use her skills to create beautiful artwork. Jack wishes for a workshop where he can create custom furniture and finally get the recognition he deserves. And Sarah wishes for a magic stethoscope that will allow her to heal the sick and help those in need.

Their wishes are granted and the friends are all able to achieve their dreams. Lucy becomes a successful artist and designer, creating beautiful pieces that are sold all over the world. Jack opens a workshop and becomes a sought-after furniture maker, creating one-of-a-kind pieces for clients all over the country. And Sarah uses her magic stethoscope to heal countless patients and make a positive impact on the world.

As the friends celebrate their success, they realize that they have all achieved their goals by using their skills and talents to make a positive difference in the world. They also realize that they have all found true happiness and fulfillment by following their passions and using their skills to help others.

The moral of "The Three Brothers" comes in handy in this scenario as it serves as a reminder that true happiness and fulfillment come from using our skills and talents to make a positive impact on the world.

CPSIA information can be obtained
at www.ICGtesting.com
Printed in the USA
LVHW060746040223
738428LV00033B/293

9 789916 676790